Samuel French Acting Edition

El Nogalar

by Tanya Saracho

SAMUELFRENCH.COM SAMUELFRENCH.CO.UK

FOR PRODUCTION ENQUIRIES

UNITED STATES AND CANADA
Info@SamuelFrench.com
1-866-598-8449

UNITED KINGDOM AND EUROPE
Plays@SamuelFrench.co.uk
020-7255-4302

Each title is subject to availability from Samuel French, depending upon country of performance. Please be aware that *EL NOGALAR* may not be licensed by Samuel French in your territory. Professional and amateur producers should contact the nearest Samuel French office or licensing partner to verify availability.

MUSIC USE NOTE

Licensees are solely responsible for obtaining formal written permission from copyright owners to use copyrighted music in the performance of this play and are strongly cautioned to do so. If no such permission is obtained by the licensee, then the licensee must use only original music that the licensee owns and controls. Licensees are solely responsible and liable for all music clearances and shall indemnify the copyright owners of the play(s) and their licensing agent, Samuel French, against any costs, expenses, losses and liabilities arising from the use of music by licensees. Please contact the appropriate music licensing authority in your territory for the rights to any incidental music.

IMPORTANT BILLING AND CREDIT REQUIREMENTS

If you have obtained performance rights to this title, please refer to your licensing agreement for important billing and credit requirements.

EL NOGALAR premiered in a production by Teatro Vista at the Goodman Theatre in Chicago, Illinois, in March 2011. The performance was directed by Cecilie D. Keenan, with sets by Brian Sidney Bembridge, and costumes by Christine Pascual. The stage manager was Rita Vreeland. The cast was as follows:

ANITA	Christina Nieves
MAITE	Charín Alvarez
VALERIA	Sandra Delgado
DUNIA	Yunuen Pardo
LOPEZ	Carlo Lorenzo Garcia

CHARACTERS

MAITE: a landowner
ANITA: Maite's daughter, twenty-three
VALERIA: Maite's eldest daughter, thirty-three
DUNIA: a maid
LOPEZ: a "merchant"

SETTING

A pecan orchard in Northern Mexico

TIME

At the dawn of the takeover by the Northern Cartels

AUTHOR'S NOTE

Every time Dunia and Lopez have a scene, the whole thing should technically be in Spanish. However, this play was created for an English-speaking audience, so a device was employed where the Dunia/Lopez scenes begin in Spanish, but then switch to English with the changing of a light source (such as clicking on a light). It's kind of like clicking on the "English Mode" or turning on the "English dial." It's just for the benefit of an English-speaking audience and should not be noted by the actors in the performance – they should seamlessly continue their Spanish action and dialogue into English

Also, / denotes a place of overlapping. The next line must come in at the /. Please observe.

Scene One

*(Natural light; however, much is able to seep in through the closed drapes. **DUNIA** is in the middle of changing the bed. She sprays air freshener as she goes in the closet to put away clean, fancy dresses, which she inspects. She comes outside and sprays some more. She is about to leave when she remembers to take **MAITE**'s earrings and bracelets out of her pocket and very carefully puts them back in their proper place. As she is doing this, **LOPEZ** enters, carrying a book.)*

LOPEZ.	DUNIA.
¿QUÉ HACES, DUNIA? / *[What are you doing, Dunia?]* Qué tanto buscas, ¿eh? *[What are you doing here in the dark, huh?]*	*(Quickly, startled.)* Ay, CHIHUAHUAS. ¡Me espantaste! *[Oh, jeez! You spooked me!]*

LOPEZ. A verda', mente cochambroza. / ¿Qué tanto esculcas? *[Ah, you see, guilty mind. What is it you're looking for?]*

DUNIA. ¿Mente que? ¡La tuya fijate! *[Guilty what? Up yours!]*

(She throws something at him.)

LOPEZ. ¿Qué buscas? *[What are you looking for?]*

DUNIA. ¡Cállate tu! ¡A ver sacate de aquí! *[Shut up! Come on, get out of here!]*

*(**DUNIA** threatens to throw something else, **LOPEZ** ducks. He clicks on the lights.)*

(Sound: Translated World.)

LOPEZ. Hey, why is everything in this house always pitch dark? / Don't you think it's a little…

DUNIA. My chest is thumping. Look at that, tun-tun, tun-tun.

>   *(Beat.)*

LOPEZ. Hey, you're not mad at me anymore! You're talking to me again.

>   *(**DUNIA** remembers that she's supposed to be ignoring him. Oh, shoot. A gesture.)*

See, I still don't understand what I did wrong! I said, "Right now is not a good time to let her go work on the border." It's the truth. You go work in one of those maquilas and what will happen? / Oh, man, I don't even want to think about it. You're better off staying here for now.

DUNIA. My mom was this close to letting me go too! *This* close. Oh, I hate you so much! Everybody wants me to be here stuck to a post. My worst nightmare is me growing old here, nailed to one of those damn pecan trees out there. I hate you so much.

LOPEZ. Don't say that, Dunia.

>   *(Pause.)*

You know, I kind of have a duty / to –

DUNIA. A duty to nothing.

LOPEZ. I only said that to your mother for your own good. A young woman alone on the border –

DUNIA. I was going with Neli, the two of us together, I wasn't going alone.

LOPEZ. Neli? That little thing with the scared little pigeon eyes?! Like sending two baby calves to a slaughter house. Like putting a sign on your forehead, "Come kidnap me and rape me, cut me into little pieces."

DUNIA. …I hate you so much.

LOPEZ. Ah, Dunita. Come on.

>   *(**DUNIA** opens the curtains; the Nuevo Leon hills and an orchard of pecan trees is revealed; both sun-beaten but splendid.)*

DUNIA. If Valeria walks by and sees us in here in the lady's room she's going to say something. Especially with us using up the electricity in the middle of the day. Well, she might not say something to you, but to me, she will say something.

LOPEZ. It's a sad state of affairs when the Galvans have to save their pennies and watch how much light they fucking use.

DUNIA. Well, it's a sad world right now.

LOPEZ. That it is.

(Beat.)

So why is your mom so formal with me all of a sudden? Last time I came to your house to visit with her, she was really quiet. She was just different. You too. Being so formal with me. Everybody's being so formal with me lately.

DUNIA. …

LOPEZ. What is that face? I'm one of us, Dunia.

DUNIA. Is that right?

LOPEZ. What do you mean, "Is that right?" Am I the guy who…who taught you how to swim when you were this big? Am I the guy who –

DUNIA. My brother taught me how to swim.

LOPEZ. Your brother and who else?

(Beat.)

Your brother and who else?

(Beat.)

DUNIA. You.

LOPEZ. So why is everyone treating me differently then?

DUNIA. Well, why do you walk around like someone put a crown on your head?

LOPEZ. A crown? You got it all wrong, little girl. I don't wear the crown. I'm just the court fool trying to keep the balls up in the air.

DUNIA. Well, you must be a very funny fool for the king on that hill to keep you around then and not cut off your head.

LOPEZ. Come again?

DUNIA. Nothing.

LOPEZ. Is that what people think of me?

DUNIA. I better finish spraying. The whole upstairs smells like a funeral home.

>   *(Starts to go.)*

LOPEZ. Fine. Then if you won't keep me company, I'm going to sit in this chair and read this book. I came up to get one of these books they have up in the study. But I thought I remembered there being more books.

DUNIA. Valeria put most of them in boxes. Who's there to read them now?

LOPEZ. She's probably read them all. She's smart that way.

>   *(He settles in the chair to read.)*

DUNIA. So you're set on reading in this room then?

LOPEZ. Yes, is that a problem?

DUNIA. No, no. I mean, if you want to sit in your dirty boots in the lady's room, / then you go ahead and sit, you know?

LOPEZ. My boots are not dirty... You like these boots? I just got them last week. You like these boots, don't you?

DUNIA. I thought by now, you'd be at the airport in Monterrey waiting for them, not sitting around reading books but what do I know.

LOPEZ. Their flight's delayed. Apparently, New York is under twenty centimeters of snow. Can you believe that? Twenty centimeters.

DUNIA. Yes, I saw it on the television.

LOPEZ. That doesn't even seem possible to me.

DUNIA. Oh, snow is like nothing to them up there.

LOPEZ. *(Takes out BlackBerry and looks at flight information.)* Then tell me why their phones are down and why this flight is two hours late, if it's like nothing to them, huh? /

(Looking for flight information.)

It says here it won't land for two more hours.

DUNIA. Show-off. You see how you are? Always showing off your new things.

LOPEZ. Oh this? You like this, huh? You want one of these don't you?

DUNIA. Show-off.

LOPEZ. See, you can look up the weather and flight info. You can look up just about anything.

(Handing it to her.)

Go ahead, look.

(She won't take it. But she wants to.)

It has a camera. And a chatting thing.

DUNIA. *(Snatches it from him.)* Let me see that thing! The things they invent nowadays. If one's got the money to buy it, you can have just about anything you want.

LOPEZ. Money is not everything.

DUNIA. *(Lowers her voice.)* Ooh, you know who you sound like?

LOPEZ. *(Lowers his.)* No I don't. I won't ever end up worried about what lights I turn on and off. And do you know why? Because I save, I save and I plan. I don't just go around wiping my ass with money like these people do!

DUNIA. *(About BlackBerry.)* Oh, you don't wipe your ass with your money? Look at you in your new snake skin boots.

(Beat.)

I don't know much, but I'd be afraid to be such a show-off around here. Find yourself shot in the back of the head. End up with your head on a post by the highway. / Aren't you scared of them, Memo? They change their mind on a whim.

LOPEZ. *(A shift, he's not joking anymore.)* Hey! Stop talking like that. You understand me, you stop talking like that. What happened to your brother – Martin was my friend, Dunia.

DUNIA. I know.

LOPEZ. He was my friend.

DUNIA. Well, your friend went and got himself killed by the maña.

LOPEZ. Don't say that word out loud, Dunia!

DUNIA. Well, he did. Got his head peeled like an apple. / Put it on a stick like a lollipop.

LOPEZ. I mean it. Don't be joking like that! What's wrong with you? What is… You need to learn to have more respect for…for things. How are you going to joke like that about your own brother? / Oh, man…that little head of yours.

> *(Beat.)*

DUNIA. What else can you do but joke? What are we all going to do? Spend the day crying? Well, no. Nobody around here cries either. They don't even let us cry. We all just walk around like we're a movie on mute. You can see people's mouths moving but all you hear is the static.

LOPEZ. I think you're a little affected in the head, baby girl. Maybe you should go talk to Father Miguel.

DUNIA. Father Miguel is the biggest Mafioso in this town! Well, besides that man on the hill up there.

LOPEZ. I'm telling you Dunia, your mouth is going to get you in a –

DUNIA. Why are you the only one they leave alone, Memo?

LOPEZ. …

DUNIA. All the men your age. Killed. Why Memo?

LOPEZ. *(Beat.)* Because I know when to keep my mouth shut which is not something I can say for you, little girl.

DUNIA. So that's all it takes to be best of friends with the maña? That doesn't seem so hard to do.

LOPEZ. For you that'd be an impossible thing to do. I need to buy you a zipper to sew on that little mouth of yours.

DUNIA. I'm going to figure out a way, Memo.

LOPEZ. Oh, no. Listen to me, don't go thinking that you're smarter than everybody else because you're not, you're just a silly little thing and I'm telling you, it will end up bad for you. Are you listening to me?

DUNIA. …

LOPEZ. This is not a game.

DUNIA. I know this is not a game! Why do you always think I'm just so stupid? I know it's not a game. But people have to do something.

LOPEZ. Dunia!

DUNIA. Wait, I'm not trying to be a hero. I don't mean *something* like that! Believe me I'm not trying to end up dismembered by a landfill. All I'm trying to do is learn to swim in it like you. Without drowning.

LOPEZ. Understand that in all of *this*, there is no way for girls like you to "figure it out." Women are zeros, you understand me? Zeros to the left. I don't want to have to start worrying about you, you hear me Dunia? I already got these fucking women coming in today and I'm going to have enough with making them get that they just can't come in here and parade about the way they used to. I'm going to have a hard enough time making them understand that we are under an occupation.

(Beat.)

Fuck, my stomach. Fuck.

(Beat.)

I send Maite email after email explaining the situation. I mean, I'm explaining it the best way I know how. With no flowery language. I am bluntly telling her that it is life or death here and every time, either she ignores it – as in she won't even reply to my fucking email or she just sends some reply asking about the river or the

fucking pecan orchard or some silly ass shit like "Does
Mrs. Garcia still make the pecan candy we love so
much?" This is some serious fucking shit we are dealing
with here and she keeps replying with questions about
pecan candy!

> *(Beat.)*

Maybe I'm just not explaining it to her correctly. But
doesn't she watch the news?!

DUNIA. Who would believe the news? To me, when I see it,
it all seems like a movie. They say on the news, "Two
men found shot to death by Los Nogales," then I walk
outside and sure enough, there they are: Two corpses
by the gates. And neither the thing I'm looking at with
my own eyes, nor the television showing close-ups of
their dead bodies – neither of those things seem real to
me. Who believes us when we tell them?

LOPEZ. Well, she better believe it or she will lose the little
she's got left. If we don't negotiate now while I got…
The Man on The Hill in a good mood, they will just come
down from the mountains and take it all by force. Why
am I telling you this? This is none of your business.

DUNIA. *(She starts to exit.)* And really, it's none of yours
either…if you think about it.

> *(She exits.)*

End of Scene

Scene Two

*(**LOPEZ** settles into the chair again.)*

LOPEZ. You're right about that. This is none of my fucking business. Ah, my fucking stomach. They need to make an actual medicine that works.

(Takes out some Mexican antacid.)

You know why I end up worrying about other people's shit? Because people don't know when to shut the fuck up around here, that's why. If I have nothing to say, I don't open my mouth. That has been my greatest gift. Zip it. Laugh when everyone else is laughing, even if you don't understand the joke, laugh anyway. And then shut your mouth. Nowadays if someone sees you open your mouth, even to take a breath, a black truck with tinted windows will come driving down the road and carry you off to the most unfortunate corners of the hills. So everybody should just shut their mouths. Half the shit people say is stupid anyway. Half the shit that people write too.

(To himself. Looking down at his book, leafing through it.)

People and their words. Words are for idle people. People who don't have to earn a living.

(Long pause as he decides on a page and attempts to read. He then becomes distracted by the room.)

This was the last room I got to see inside this house... we were never allowed upstairs. Well, the playroom, we were only allowed inside the playroom if we were bringing things up or moving furniture, but never the master bedroom. I always thought this room would be bigger, with draperies everywhere and maybe with gold things on the walls or something. But when I finally made it upstairs and came in to see it...

(Beat.)

Yeah, you always think things are better on the other side when the door is closed on you. You imagine it in your head with more color or something. Like this bed. Everyone talked about this bed so much…the *Porfirio Díaz Bed! It belonged to Porfirio Díaz… Porfirio Díaz himself slept on it!* So you think "Oh, well the bed of a president must be better and bigger than normal people's beds," you know? It must be embedded with gold, dripping with diamonds and shit. But then you finally see the bed and well, it's just a bed. It's a nice bed. It's big and with a nice design. But it remains just an old bed.

> *(He goes to it and tests it. Bounces on it a bit then lies on it, book on his chest.)*

The Porfirio Díaz bed…

> *(He begins to doze off as lights transition to the next scene.)*

End of Scene

Scene Three

(**VALERIA** *is in the playroom; at least we think it's
the playroom, because it seems to also serve as some
kind of storage room. There are boxes everywhere,
and things under sheets and tarps. One of those
covered treasures is a rustic rocking horse, made
of porous pecan wood.* **VALERIA** *is sitting with
these covered artifacts, looking out the window,
fingering a ring of keys. The lights are not on, and
the only light coming in is natural light seeping
through the windows.* **DUNIA** *enters, carrying the
rag and spray bottle she had with her in the master
bedroom. She clicks on the lights [Real World:
English/Spanish].*)

VALERIA. ¡CÚANTAS VECES LES TENGO QUE DECIR
QUE NO PRENDAN LA LUZ / SI TODAVÍA HAY LUZ
AFUERA! *[HOW MANY TIMES DO I HAVE TO TELL
YOU NOT TO TURN ON THE LIGHTS IF THERE IS
STILL LIGHT OUTSIDE!]*

DUNIA. ¡Ay, oiga! ¡Ay, no asuste! ¡Ya pues, la apagamos
entonces! *[Oh, don't scare me. Alright then, we'll turn it off
then!]*

> (*Makes a big gesture of turning off the light.
> [Trans: English]*)

There, light off.

> (*Holding on to the threshold.*)

VALERIA. How many times do I say it? We don't need all the
lights in the daytime.

> (*Notices* **DUNIA** *hasn't come in.*)

What are you doing?

DUNIA. (*Shakes her head to say "Nothing."*) …

VALERIA. Duniacomehere.

DUNIA. …huh?

> (**DUNIA** *goes to* **VALERIA**.)

VALERIA. What did you do to your face?

DUNIA. Nothing.

VALERIA. What did you do?

DUNIA. I didn't do anything to my face.

VALERIA. You look like a cockroach in a bakery.

DUNIA. I just put on a little powder.

VALERIA. You look like you dunked your head in flour.

DUNIA. *(Politely.)* I do not. My cousin Mila brought it from McAllen from a department store. It's made for my color.

VALERIA. Yes, but you have to go and test the colors on your face, she can't just read a color that sounds like it might go with your skin and hope it works. You have to try it on.

DUNIA. Mila and I are the same color, and it looks perfect on her. I don't think it looks bad.

> *(Beat.)*

Just that nobody around here ever fixes themselves up so you're not used to it.

> *(Beat.)*

VALERIA. Well, you look ridiculous.

DUNIA. Well…

> *(Better she shut her mouth.)*

VALERIA. The flight is delayed. Now they'll get here when it's dark and we'll have to drive through their checkpoints in the dark – because now these people have decided to erect checkpoints wherever they please! Oh, God I did not want to drive back in the dark.

DUNIA. Yeah, Memo told me the airplane is delayed two hours.

VALERIA. He did? Is he here?

> *(DUNIA nods.)*

You shouldn't call him that.

DUNIA. Everybody calls him that.

VALERIA. Yes, but I don't think he likes it anymore. I think he wants us to call him by his name now.

DUNIA. That is his name. That's what anyone's ever called him and now he wants us to start calling him something else?

VALERIA. Just say Guillermo. Better yet, call him Mr. Lopez.

DUNIA. I'm sorry, but I'm not going to call him Mr. Lopez. You know what Mr. Lopez is doing right now? Mr. Lopez is currently in the master bedroom sniffing around.

VALERIA. He's what?

DUNIA. I found him there roaming like he was *Peter through his house.*

VALERIA. What is he doing up here?

DUNIA. That's what I wanted to know. He said he was looking for a book to read. Ha! Like he's ever read a book in his life.

VALERIA. Dunia.

DUNIA. I'm sorry but you know you think the same as me. I'm just saying what I see.

VALERIA. Well…stop seeing things…and go and tell him that…ah, go and ask him if he wants a drink.

DUNIA. You go ask him.

(A look from **VALERIA.***)*

I mean, maybe *you* should ask him, you know? So the two of you can –

VALERIA. So we can what?

DUNIA. You know…so you two can *talk.*

VALERIA. And what will I say to him? I'm already thinking about this agonizing drive we're going to take to Monterrey. He never says a word!

DUNIA. I don't know…maybe ask him to teach you again about how to chat on the computer.

VALERIA. No. We treat him as if he still worked here. And it's absolutely embarrassing. We should have the money to have people do these things.

(Beat.)

VALERIA. What are you looking at me like that for?

> (DUNIA *makes an "I'm not looking at you" gesture.*)

You look ridiculous with your hair like that.

DUNIA. Like how? This is how they wear it on MTV.

VALERIA. You watch the satellite too much.

DUNIA. Not anymore. No more satellite. Now how else am I going to learn about the world in this little town?

VALERIA. Enough talking! Go and make sure you sweep all around the house. Especially the porch.

DUNIA. Fulgencio already went around doing that in the morning.

VALERIA. Poor old man, you let him bend his back to do that?

DUNIA. He wanted to do it. You know he's hungry for something to do. He sits by the front door like this *(Demonstrates.)* just looking ahead like one of those London soldiers.

VALERIA. Still you should supervise him so he doesn't break a hip.

> *(Beat.)*

Should I change? Maybe I should change into something else. No, this is fine.

DUNIA. Maybe put on something more lively?

VALERIA. Like what?

DUNIA. I don't know. Like with color. Or like with flowers or something.

VALERIA. I'm not going to go around looking like I belong in a circus, thank you very much.

> *(Exiting.)*

No, I think this will be fine…

> *(VALERIA exits.)*

DUNIA. *(Straightening up.)* Please, they wouldn't even let you sell tickets at the circus. You'd depress the clowns, make the monkeys cry. Please, God, if I ever look like that when I'm her age and let all this go to waste *(Referencing her body.)* shoot me like that, in my head.

    (Shoots her head with her finger.)

End of Scene

Scene Four

(**LOPEZ** *enters.*)

LOPEZ. I fell asleep in there. That Porfirio Díaz bed is a trap. / You sink right in.

DUNIA. *(Under her breath.)* …Shameless. So shameless.

LOPEZ. How long was I down for? Why didn't you wake me up?

DUNIA. Oh, now I'm your alarm clock too? You weren't even asleep for ten minutes you just –

> *(A great commotion is heard. We hear dogs barking, car doors opening and closing, a bag being dropped, and just the general feel of an arrival.* **LOPEZ** *goes for his piece. Yes, old boy is packing, okay? But just don't make a big deal out of it ever. This is just what the men do now.* **DUNIA** *notices.)*

DUNIA. NO. I think that's them. Put that thing away!

LOPEZ. How is that them? That can't be them, their flight is –

DUNIA. I don't know, / but I think it is!

> *(***LOPEZ** *hides the gun again and runs down the stairs. On the way down, he meets* **VALERIA** *on the landing, who's just appeared. They kind of awkwardly greet each other, and he exits out the front door. Guess it has started to get a little dark without us noticing. [Still English].)*

VALERIA. Memo, I didn't know you – I mean Guillermo. Oh yeah. Go, go.

LOPEZ. Eh, I'm going to help with the –

> *(Dusk. There are no lights on inside the house, but something's going on outside with the car's headlights.* **DUNIA** *puts down the rag and the Febreze bottle, and as she's about to go out the door,* **VALERIA** *stops her. All this happens fast and has a tinge of chaos.)*

VALERIA. What's going on?

DUNIA. I think it's them. I think they got here early after all.

> *(Beat.)*

VALERIA. But they were delayed two hours!

> (**DUNIA** *shrugs her shoulders.*)

Well, go help them with their things! And turn on the lights for God's sake!

> (**DUNIA** *turns on the lights. [Real Time: Spanish/ English].*)

DUNIA. Ah, sí ahora sí prendemos la luz, ¿verdad?

VALERIA. ¡Ándale / ve!

> (**VALERIA** *comes down the steps slowly as we hear the next exchange of voices coming from outside.*)

LOPEZ. A ver, ¡Fulgencio! Las maletas. Yo les ayudo con esto, no se preocupen, yo les ayudo.

MAITE. *(Offstage.)* ¡Memo! ¿Eres tú Memo? No te reconozco... Anis, do you remember Memo? Dios Santo, look at my orchard Anita! I feel like running / por El Nogalar this instant. ¿Y estos perros? I don't recognize these dogs. Oh, your allergies are going to kill you if he's an inside dog Anita.

ANITA. *(Offstage.)* Mom, seriously don't start with that. Mom...Mom please don't start. Jesus Christ! Can you just stop acting crazy and come inside with us please? Can somebody please go make sure she doesn't fall flat on her ass please? However you say it...¡ve con ella! Please.

> (**ANITA** *enters the foyer;* **DUNIA** *trails her with bags.*)

Oh, God...it's just like...like a fucking freak show everywhere we go. And there goes that little old man chasing after her. He's going to break something.

DUNIA. Salio volando la Señora.

    (Beat.)

ANITA. Yeah.

    (Beat.)

VALERIA. Anita.

ANITA. Oh, my God, Vale.

    (They hug long and hard.)

Vale…

VALERIA. Párale si no voy a llorar, eh.

ANITA. Vale…

VALERIA. *(Tenderly.)* ¿Ya, no? Anita…

    (They have a little moment. These sisters haven't seen each other in a while.)

¿Y Mami?

ANITA. She ran off like a maniac of course. Oh, God Vale, she kept crying and acting crazy at the stopover in Houston so I gave her a little pill to calm her down but I think it just made her more crazy.

VALERIA. ¿Cómo qué se fue corriendo? She can't go out like that when it is getting dark.

ANITA. Well, I don't know. Go get her then.

VALERIA. Ay, ya empezamos. Ahorita regreso. Dunia, lleva esto para arriba, por favor. *[Ah, here we go. I'll be right back. Dunia, take this upstairs please.]*

DUNIA. Sí para alla iba. *[Yeah, that's where I was going.]*

VALERIA. Ya estás en casa hermanita.

    (Exit.)

ANITA. Am I? I guess this is home now, huh?

    *(A pause. **ANITA** contemplates the house. The exhaustion is super evident; she is mad tired. After a while she notices **DUNIA**.)*

Hola.

DUNIA. Hello.

ANITA. Nice. Hi.

(Beat.)

Warning, *Hola* is as much as you're going to get from me, okay? My Spanish is... No hablo el Español muy –

DUNIA. Ah, don't worry. Do not worry you. I have been practicing very much.

ANITA. Great. Awesome. I mean, I'll understand everything you say, I just can't... Yeah.

(Beat.)

I'm beyond tired. Do you know which room I'm –

DUNIA. Oh, yes. Come, te instalamos in the pink room. Vale she said the pink room.

ANITA. I don't care where you put me at this point, as long as there's a freakin' bed.

DUNIA. Ah, pues...la Señorita Valeria. This is the room of boxes now.

ANITA. The room of boxes? Why is this the room of... Oh, I can't think about it right now. I'm seriously dying of exhaustion. I just want a bed and I want sleep.

DUNIA. You would like a coffee?

ANITA. No, thank you Dunia. Then I won't sleep. I want to actually sleep.

DUNIA. I can't...even laugh that you are here. You left when you were more young but I have very pretty memories of when we played.

ANITA. What? You don't have to speak... I mean, you can say it in Spanish. I understand everything, I just... I'm self-conscious about my accent.

DUNIA. No, you are my only opportunity to practice. I tell you that I want to have a proficiency.

ANITA. Alright, you can practice with me so you can have your proficiency.

DUNIA. Oh, that's very good. I have not before told you but I want to leave from here and go to live in the United States.

ANITA. Why? Don't you know we're all coming back?

I'm hungry. I want some flautas. The food is like one of my constant...it's the thing I remember the most. And this room. Will you go and ask what's her name for me, please Dunia?

DUNIA. The cook, Tere? Ya no está Tere. *[Tere is not here anymore.]*

ANITA. Where did she go?

DUNIA. Se murió – *[She died –]* ah, she died the last year.

ANITA. Oh, no. That's terrible. Nobody tells me these things.

DUNIA. Yes, the last year. Of neumony.

> *(Beat.)*

Pulmony?

ANITA. That's so sad.

DUNIA. Yes.

> *(Beat.)*

ANITA. *(About a typical Mexican toy.)* Wow. Look at this thing. I always used to get these ribbons tangled when I was a kid. God, it's like time skips over this house. Everything stays the same.

DUNIA. Not everything. Everything is different now. In the town, in Los Nogales. It is different.

ANITA. Different how?

DUNIA. I let Valeria or somebody tell. Wait a minute, I will get the hang. You know I wasn't waiting until you come so I practice the English.

ANITA. Look how tall the trees look from here.

DUNIA. Yes, they are tall now. Nobody who cut them.

ANITA. They're not as green as I remember. Even though I never thought... I never thought this orchard was much to look at. It was fun to hide in and run through, but...but it's what we've got, right?

> *(Beat.)*

Oh, my God I'm exhausted.

DUNIA. Entonces is good you come early, ¿verdad?

ANITA. Totally. We would have been like stranded for two hours if it wasn't for that guy Pedro who was so sweet to bring us all the way home.

(She's uncovered a doll.)

Oh, my God. This was my doll!

(Beat.)

DUNIA. Pedro Treviño?

ANITA. Yeah, that's his name, right? Pedro. The teacher guy.

(Beat.)

Rosita! This doll's name was Rosita!

(Intimately to the doll.)

DUNIA. Pedro Treviño is not a teacher guy anymore.

(VALERIA has entered. She's not too happy with DUNIA's talk of Pedro.)

VALERIA. Dunia. A Mami se le antojo cafe. Con canela, como le gusta. Ándale. *[Go make the coffee, go on. Mami has a taste for it – Go.]*

DUNIA. Voy. *[Going]*

(Exits with a knowing look to ANITA.)

VALERIA. No la aguanto. Es insoportable. *[I can't stand her. She's insufferable.]*

(Beat.)

ANITA. Look, Vale! This was my favorite doll.

VALERIA. They are all here. Every one.

ANITA. Why are they all in boxes? Why does this make me want to cry?

VALERIA. You are tired.

ANITA. We haven't slept. Mami was on an *up* the whole way.

VALERIA. *(Lovingly grabbing her face, petting her hair.)* You are home, hermanita – Look at you, Anis. You are here.

ANITA. Yeah.

VALERIA. I know it has been so very hard for you this year. Let me tell you, it was the loneliest Christmas here.

ANITA. See…don't say those things to me, Vale. It makes me feel guilty for getting to be over there, closer to Mami.

VALERIA. No, no te lo digo por eso, Chiquita. *[No, that's not why I say it, baby girl.]* It's just the way it is, right? I am just… I am just happy to see you. It has been such a long time without seeing you.

ANITA. Vale, you see me when we Skype.

VALERIA. Oh, I hate that thing.

ANITA. It was a hot mess, Vale.

VALERIA. No, me lo imagino. *[No, I can imagine.]*

ANITA. No one has gotten any sleep with this big final opus of a fight she had with *you know who.*

VALERIA. Te hacemos un tesito. *[We can make you a bit of tea.]*

ANITA. No, Vale. I'm trying to tell you that she's not okay. I don't see her for almost six months, we hardly talk on the phone even and then out of the blue, one day she comes to get me at school.

She comes on a random Tuesday with no warning. Wild eyed and super hyper and she just goes and pulls me out of school, just like that. We drive into New York and her mouth doesn't stop. We get there and she's living – because I don't know if you know, Vale, but she lost the loft downtown. She sold it and still managed to have no money for my tuition. You think I don't know that this is why she took me out of school?

VALERIA. Anis –

ANITA. Why is she always a fucking mess?! She lost her passport, now the cell phone, we almost didn't have money to get here. We had to fly economy class! / I don't even want to tell you where we were staying. This man she's living with, he pretends to be this intellectual, but he's just a fucking meathead. He treats her like a servant. He says things about her being Mexican. Things like I've never heard before about us. People don't talk about us that way.

VALERIA. I'm sorry, Anis.

Please, don't tell me these things.

ANITA. He does. When he says the word "Mexican" it sounds like he's saying a bad word. Like he's saying "shit" or something. I don't know how to explain it.

VALERIA. You know he means other kind of Mexicans. You know what he means. He doesn't mean us.

ANITA. Fucking idiot.

(Pause.)

Vale, I think Mami stays because she has no other place to go.

VALERIA. No me digas eso, por favor.

ANITA. I'm worried, Vale. He took all our money. / He drained her. Oh, don't cry Vale. I'm not saying it so you'll cry. I'm saying it because I haven't been able to talk to anyone about this. I'm saying it because, because I'm home right? I'm home and just want to sleep for two days and go back to being myself. Go back to not worrying about anything.

(Beat.)

VALERIA. *(Starts to cry.)* I know… I know.

You should rest.

(Pause.)

ANITA. Has he proposed to you?

VALERIA. ¿Quién?

ANITA. What do you mean "quién?" Memo.

*(***VALERIA** *shakes her head.)*

Well, what are you waiting for?

VALERIA. What can I do? Propose to him myself? Oh, the whole thing is so embarrassing. Every woman we know is married, it seems. I'm the only...hasta a Dunia le han propuesto matrimonio. *[Even* **DUNIA** *has had offers of marriage.]* She's got an accountant, a butcher and a man who fixes cars, after her. Like flies she's got them after her. ¿Y yo? I do not even have this one man that everyone says...this one man who is the whole reason I stayed in Los – Oh, it makes me sick to be around him. I start shaking. I don't know if it's anger or just pure – I don't know.

ANITA. He loves you, Vale. It's always been so obvious. And the way he's kept watch over you and over Los Nogales. It's obvious.

VALERIA. Is it? If it is so obvious, what is he waiting for? No, he doesn't even notice I am alive. No sé... When Papi died, I came here because there was something safe about knowing Memo would be around but –

ANITA. Okay, let's not talk about dads in this room. It makes me miss mine. Why do men die?

VALERIA. *(A moment of tenderness between them.)* Sometimes I think I imagined the whole thing. All those letters.

ANITA. Letters are so romantic. Who writes letters anymore?

VALERIA. Well, he wrote letters. The entire time I lived in England, he wrote me. He wrote me these long – well, I've shown you, these long nonsense letters that maybe you'd think a fourth grader had written, but to me they were...they were Los Nogales to me. Pedacitos de él, de esta tierra, del aire.

      (Beat.)

Ey, Anita, por favor no le comentes – *[Hey, Anita, please don't tell –]* don't tell Mami about the letters okay?

ANITA. Okay.

VALERIA. She's always been strange about Memo... I don't know.

ANITA. Yeah, I know.

VALERIA. I'm not imagining it, right?

ANITA. But he's like doing really well, right? Isn't he like a big /... That's good for you, Vale. He'll take care of you.

VALERIA. Yes, he owns a lot of property now. A lot. He can't even look at me in the face, how is going to then take care of me?

(**MAITE** *calls out as she's racing up the stairs.*)

MAITE. ¡NIÑAS! NENAS ¿DÓNDE SE METIERON? ¡NIÑAS! *[GIRLS! WHERE DID YOU GO? GIRLS!]*

(**MAITE** *enters, out of breath. Her boots are muddy and her hair a bit disheveled, but she is a vision. She is quite beautiful. Regal in an approachable sort of way.*)

There you are, mi Vale. Vale, the nogalar is completely dry! Hasta de noche se puede uno dar cuenta de lo seco que están esos árboles. *[My pecan trees are completely dry! Even at night you can see how dry they are.]* My mother would weep right now!

VALERIA. Mami cómo quieres que –

MAITE. AY, MIS HIJAS!

(*Contemplates both her daughters.*)

Dios Mio, ya parezco La Llorona. Come here, Vale. Ven te digo. Mis dos hijas together at last. How long since you saw each other? Over a year?

VALERIA. Three years, Mami.

MAITE. Three whole years! Mi pobre, Valeria, tan demacrada. *[My poor Valeria, so weathered.]* Look at these bags under your eyes, mi Vale. I have an excellent cream for this. Don't you worry.

(*Hugging* **VALERIA.**)

But why so skinny? Look at her tiny little wrists, Anita. Estás hecha un hueso, Vale. It's all my fault. I'm starving you aren't I?

VALERIA. Pues, tú sí que te ves hermosa, Mama. Como siempre. *[Well, you do look beautiful, Mom. Like always.]*

MAITE. De qué hablas, estoy hecha un asco! *[What are you talking about, I'm disgusting!]* Look at me. I'm all wrinkles and sagging skin.

VALERIA. No, you look amazing, Mami.

MAITE. We do look like we could be sisters, don't we?

ANITA. Mami, your boots. They're full of mud.

MAITE. Oh, they're just boots! Ay, here. I'll take them off. Probably should throw them away, they're all wet. I think they're ruined.

VALERIA. No, Mama. / We'll clean them.

MAITE. *(Interrupting.)* Pero ve esto por favor! Mi cuarto de jugetes! Mi niñez. *[But will you look at this! My playroom! My childhood.]* ¿Pero por qué lo tienen en este estado, Valeria Guadalupe? *[But why do you have it in this state, Valeria Guadalupe?]* This is an apocalyptic disaster zone!

> *(She begins to uncover things quite dramatically.* **VALERIA** *and* **ANITA** *react vocally: "Mama, por favor el polvo." ["Jesus, Mom. My fucking allergies," etc.])*

Awake! Awake my friends! ¡Es hora de despertarse! *[It's time to wake up.]*

> *(She has uncovered all but one treasure. She becomes distracted by some dolls.)*

Mis muñecas. Look at this, Ana Maria. This was one of my first dolls. They don't make dolls like this anymore.

> *(She unearths an even older doll.)*

Hello old friend. Have you been forgotten under all this dust?

> *(She is on the floor with an armful of dolls.)*

ANITA. Mom, I think that one was mine.

MAITE. Really? Well, here you go then. Now you two are reunited.

> *(Beat.)*

Wait. Where's the...where's my horse. Dónde está el caballito de Madera –

(She unearths a beautiful brown rocking horse, a bit weathered, but still showing some signs of its former majesty.)

ANITA. *(Under her breath.)* Oh, fuck. Tavito's horse.

MAITE. No. Not Gustavito's horse. This was my grandfather's horse. My great-grandfather had it made for him from two Nogales. I never told you that, did I? Pecan is not good for these kinds of things, too porous, pero el bisabuelo wouldn't hear "no." We've been a family who hasn't understood the word "no." He was always so proud of this orchard, of those trees and – Look at you my old friend.

(Some crying.)

We've gotten old haven't we? Forgotten, tú y yo. I wish you would have seen this in all its glory, Anis.

ANITA. I remember the horse, Mom.

MAITE. I used to play for hours in this room. This room was glorious. We had an entire wall of music boxes because my mother – I wonder if there are any of them left. She collected them from her trips to Europe and South America. She had one from Martinique con una negrita asi...que se movía así...

(She does a quick hip dance.)

Why do we forget the things that matter? Look at this place now. It breaks my heart in two. Is there any going back now?

(Pause.)

VALERIA. You must be so tired...

MAITE. Anis...

(Beat.)

Mi bolsa por favor.

ANITA. No, Mami. She wants to take some pills that make her loopy and I already gave her something I shouldn't have. She should just go to bed.

VALERIA. ¿Por qué mejor no te duermes, Mama? *[Why don't you go to sleep instead, Mom?]*

MAITE. I'm not tired. I could do jumping jacks right now.

(**DUNIA** *enters with coffee.*)

Ah, Dunia. Pero no puede ser lo cuanto has crecido Dunia. *[Ah, Dunia. But it can't be how much you've grown Dunia.]*

(*To* **ANITA** *and* **VALERIA.**)

She was this big when I left. Y tan guapa Dunia. *[And so attractive Dunia.]*

DUNIA. Favor que usted me hace. *[You're too kind.]*

MAITE. Just look at her.

ANITA. Mami, don't drink the coffee please. You won't sleep.

MAITE. Dunia, estas dos aburridas me quieren mandar a la cama, pero que se vayan muchísimo a la chingada. *[Dunia, these two bores want to send me to bed, but they go straight to hell.]* You go to bed, you old ladies. The night is for the living!

DUNIA. El Señor Lopez la está esperando abajo. ¿Qué disque que tiene que hablar con usted muy urgentemente? *[Mr. Lopez is waiting for you downstairs. He said something about needing to speak to you urgently?]*

MAITE. (*To* **VALERIA.**) Who?

VALERIA. Memo. Guillermo Lopez, Mami.

MAITE. Ah, Memo! Yes!

(*Quick beat, it's something.*)

Ese Memo. How handsome he's gotten. Envarnecio, eh. *[He's filled out, huh.]*

(*To* **VALERIA.**)

Valeria, mas vale que te pongas las pilas, ¡mi amor! *[Valeria, you better get with it, my love!]* I want to be a grandma before I'm too old.

(Exiting.)

A ver qué quiere el distinguido Senor Lopez. *[Let's go see what the distinguished Mr. Lopez wants.]*

(Beat. They exit.)

VALERIA. Why did she act as if she didn't remember Memo at first?

ANITA. Prepare yourself again for the mysteries of Mami. Speaking of Memo, why did he leave us stranded at the airport? If it hadn't been for that Pedro / we would still be there.

VALERIA. Memo didn't leave you stranded; we thought you were coming in later. You know, I have a strong feeling that it wasn't a coincidence that Pedro was there. He was waiting for you. Pedro is not... Pedro is maña. Es un sicario and a very dangerous man to have around.

ANITA. Maña like the...?

VALERIA. YES.

ANITA. My brother's teacher is now maña?

VALERIA. YES!

ANITA. He doesn't look maña.

VALERIA. And what does maña look like?

ANITA. Like, you know...like with dark sunglasses and guns. Like Scarface.

VALERIA. Por Dios, Ana Maria! Claro que no.

ANITA. Like scary. Pedro didn't look scary to me.

VALERIA. Well be scared. We are all contaminated here. They look like you and me now. The economy has made good boys, from good families todos mañosos. And the nacos too of course. The ones who've been waiting to have a little something, the ones who grew up with nothing, those are the bloodiest and most cruel. Anita, let's do this tomorrow. Please. There's a lot to say and a lot to plan.

ANITA. I don't understand anything.

VALERIA. I know you don't. Tomorrow. For tonight, just... duerme con los angelitos. *[Sleep with the angels.]*

ANITA. Yeah, fine. I'm not... I'm not going to worry about it tonight.

> *(Starts to go.)*

I am exhausted. I feel forty years old all of a sudden.

VALERIA. Forty is not so old.

ANITA. What are you talking about, forty is ancient.

> *(ANITA exits.)*

VALERIA. ¿Y veintinueve?

> *(VALERIA is left staring, sadly taking in the nursery. She then snaps out of it and remembers the electricity is being wasted. She abruptly turns off the light. We see the orchard and hills in the moonlight as she exits.)*

End of Scene

Scene Five

(**LOPEZ** *enters. He's carrying his keys and his
BlackBerry. He clicks on the electronic key to unlock
his Escalade but doesn't go. The headlights have
come on. He pops a Tums in his mouth.*)

LOPEZ. *(To himself.)* Fucking shit.

(Beat.)

I just made no sense. I sounded like a fucking idiot
just now. Moron! Maite comes down, looking all...she
comes down and I start stuttering. I can look at Chato
straight in the face and not stutter once but this woman
comes down the stairs and I can't say consonants all of
a sudden. And the way she just looked at me. Like she's
about to pet her little dog. Why am I even here panting,
offering my help? Letting her give me those looks that –

(Beat.)

But at least she looked at me, right? My God, she hasn't
changed a bit. If anything she's more beautiful now.
God, her eyes. Those lips. A person can't make sense
in front of someone like that. It's like you're in front
of a...

(Beat.)

What if I just go in there and try to explain it again to
her. Draw it in crayons for her so she understands that
she will lose every-fucking-thing she owns if she doesn't
jump on this because the clock is ticking on their offer.
Five years ago this offer might have been ridiculous, but
the way things are today, it is as generous as it's going
to get. The fact that she even gets an offer is short of a
miracle really! Every other piece of land around here
has just been taken by force. I need to paint a picture
for her that breaks it all down. And I'm going to need
to get Chato something big. iPad. Yeah, I'll get him a
couple of iPads.

(Pause.)

Tomorrow. Tomorrow I'll come and explain it better.

(His BlackBerry rings.)

Ah, fuck me. Fuck me. Hello? Ey, Chato! How are... what? I know, I'm a motherfucker. I'll come to the next one. You know poker's not my thing, you guys will just clean me out anyway but... Who? Oh, yeah, she's here, they're all back. Yeah, I was going to go get them myself but your boy Pedro gave them a ride. Oh, well, thank you for that. That was very nice of you to send an escort – What? Yes. Thank you.

(Beat.)

No, I didn't get a chance to. Maybe we should give her a little bit of time to say hello and goodbye to things. Ah, NO PLEASE CHATO. Let me. As a personal favor to me. Yes. I'll get it all sorted out. Thank you, Chato. Oh, hey I know we were talking about those iPads the other day and I'd love it if you let me bring you a couple, you know for you and your kid. Yeah, you know the iPad 2's that just came out? Yeah. Come on, after all you've... Yeah, I know. You're right, Chato. I'm a motherfucker.

(Laughs a little too loud.)

Yeah, alright. Tomorrow then. Alright then.

(He hangs up.)

Fucking shit.

(He clicks on the auto-start and exits to get into his truck. Sounds of him driving away. Kinda fast.)

End of Scene

Scene Six

*(The next morning. **VALERIA** enters the master
bedroom looking for **MAITE**. The bed is unmade
and one suitcase looks gutted, open-faced.)*

VALERIA. Mami...

(Beat.)

¿Mamita? No te quiero despertar pero ten ha dejado
este señor como diez mensajes... Mami? *[Mommy?
I don't want to wake you but this man has left you like ten
messages.]*

*(**ANITA** storms in and throws herself on the bed.)*

ANITA. If I wasn't starving to death I would have stayed
inside that purple bed all day and all night and all day
and all night and... Can we talk about what a good
night's sleep I had? And can we also talk about how
freakin' comfortable this bed is? Oh, my God I could
just melt right now. Melt into the Porfirio Díaz bed.
I wonder if Porfirio Díaz snored when he slept on
this bed. He might have snored and drooled himself
because it is so fucking luscious!

VALERIA. Why do people say this was Porfirio Díaz' bed?

ANITA. What?

VALERIA. I hear people say that sometimes.

ANITA. This wasn't Porfirio Díaz' bed?

VALERIA. No! Why would people think that?

ANITA. Everyone calls it the Porfirio Díaz bed. For as long
as I can remember.

VALERIA. This is from the TIMES of Porfirio Díaz. De esa
época. But he didn't actually sleep on this bed. Who
started that rumor?

ANITA. My world is shattering. So this wasn't his – he never
actually slept on this bed?

VALERIA. Ana Maria. Mami told you this, didn't she? ¿Por qué inventa cuentos? *[Why does she invent tall tales?]* She's always making up stories.

ANITA. So no Porfirio Díaz?

VALERIA. No.

ANITA. How depressing! And this whole time I would talk about it like it was part of history. Like he was part of our family or something.

VALERIA. Por Dios, Anita.

ANITA. This shows you I know nothing. My whole world is one big giant lie.

>   *(Beat.)*

Where is Mami, that big fat liar?

VALERIA. Yo juraba que estaba aquí en su recámara. *[I swore she was in here.]*

ANITA. Check the closet.

VALERIA. ¿Cómo qué "Check the closet"? ¿Qué va a estar haciendo en el closet? *[What is she going to be doing in the closet?]*

>   *(Beat.)*

ANITA. *(Laughing.)* Hey, you never know with Mami.

VALERIA. ¿Dónde estará? *[Where could she be?]*

ANITA. Vale, are we going to be homeless? / Mami doesn't know if we have money to keep this place.

VALERIA. Ay, Ana don't say those things.

ANITA. Are we?

VALERIA. I don't know. Not if Memo helps us.

ANITA. You think Mami will take his money, Vale? You know she's particular.

VALERIA. You mean she's too proud? No, why wouldn't she take his money?

ANITA. I don't know. Because she says that he's mixed up in all that nonsense with those people. The drug people.

VALERIA. He's not mixed up with… Of course she'll explain it to you like that! Is this what she said to you? It's always absolutes with Mami. It's so easy to look at it from up there and take a black and white picture of it, isn't it? Ana, it's so much more complicated than that. The only reason I can still live here without being bothered, is because of Memo.

ANITA. What about our friends? They can help us.

VALERIA. What friends?

ANITA. Grandfather was governor. We must still have some friends.

VALERIA. There are no friends left, Anita! All the people like us sold their lands and moved to Monterrey a long long time ago or you know…were burned and shot out of their homes. Se ha puesto tan feo. *[It's gotten so ugly.]*

ANITA. You are becoming as dramarama as Mami. I swear.

VALERIA. *(She starts to cry a little bit.)* You don't fully comprehend what is happening here, Ana Maria! And I don't know if I have the energy to explain it. They've taken our Mexico. They've taken our every days, our nights.

ANITA. Oh, don't start crying. I'm sorry, Vale. You're right, I'm totally not understanding what it's been like to stay here. / I'm sorry.

    (Beat.)

VALERIA. It's not the staying here…

ANITA. See, I'm worthless. Now I made you cry.

VALERIA. I get like this lately. No me hagas caso. *[Don't pay me any mind.]*

    (Beat.)

How I wish you didn't have to worry about all this. How I wish we could marry you off to a proper Mexican.

ANITA. Who wants to be married to a proper anything right now? Please.

VALERIA. Well, some women do.

(**MAITE** *enters. She's wearing running gear, her hair is in a ponytail.*)

MAITE. There is not one human being in this entire house that can make me some breakfast and a cup of coffee?

VALERIA. Ay, es que Tere falleció. *[Oh, it's because Tere died.]*

MAITE. I know, God rest her soul. She was a good cook.

VALERIA. Where did you go, Mami?

MAITE. Oh, I just had the most wonderful jog around the orchard. Cruze todo el nogalar, then I went jogging up the side of the mountain.

VALERIA. Mami you can't go up to the hills anymore. It's not safe.

ANITA. Oh, she won't listen. She'll run in those skimpy shorts even during the winter. She just likes to show off her butt.

MAITE. *(Lightly.)* Huerca malcriada...

    (Beat.)

But it's true. I will not let myself go, mi amor. Plus, for my sanity, I've got to run. And don't think that now that I'm back to take the reins of this place I will stop running, eh. I'm going to have us all running here. Get rid of that little cottage cheese you were developing at school, Anita.

ANITA. Mom!

    (Beat.)

MAITE. You know what? I think I want to eat al fresco today.

VALERIA. *(To* **MAITE.***)* ¿Quieres desayunar huevos o quieres ya almorzar algo mas fuerte?

MAITE. Pedro's here. / He was following me.

VALERIA. Ay, Dios Santo.

MAITE. At first I thought I was imagining it. "Who is this following me?" I thought. And then I turn and it was Pedro, right where the river turns. / I yell, "Ándale! You want to race? I'm warning you that I'm fast!" But he just stood there, just... And then he fell to his knees like if someone had taken the batteries out of his back. I hadn't noticed where he was standing.

VALERIA. Mami, ¿te hizo algo? *[Mom, did he do something to you?]*

MAITE. He was standing right where he was when he took Gustavo from… In that exact same place by the edge of the water…he was carrying my baby boy in his arms. His wet little body across Pedro's arms. Fifteen years I went away so I wouldn't have to think of that day.

(Breaks down a little bit.)

Why didn't I think I'd see ghosts? You and Pedro are the only ones who saw, Ana Maria.

ANITA. Don't. Stop, Mom. / Seriously.

MAITE. Le tengo mucho cariño a Pedro. He's a good boy. What am I saying? He's a man now.

VALERIA. Mami, don't get confused about Pedro. He is a beast, not a man.

MAITE. Our lives were so different then. Things made sense. People knew their place and you knew where you belonged. Our lives were simple. And then I don't know what happened. These past fifteen years since I've been gone I find the world so confusing. The world is now a version I don't recognize. We don't belong up there, we don't belong down here. Where do we fit? No encajamos. There's no place for people like us in the world anymore. The world is made of new money, of Facebook money.

(Beat.)

VALERIA. Mami, we have to have a conversation about Pedro.

MAITE. Oh, I don't want to hear nonsense and chisme right now, Valeria. You know what? I think I want to go put some flowers in Gustavito's tomb. What do you say Anita, want to come put flowers in your brother's tomb?

(Beat. **ANITA** *doesn't answer.)*

VALERIA. I will go with you.

MAITE. You'll have to see his tomb sooner or later, Anita.

ANITA. No I won't.

VALERIA. What did Memo want to talk about? Is he going to help us?

MAITE. Ah, no quiero tocar ese tema! I don't want us spending any time thinking about it. I just got here and I'm already bombarded with Memo and his asinine offers to lend us money / which will do I don't know what exactly! I'm bombarded with Valeria's rants about the mafia y no se que tanta cosa…

VALERIA. Did he offer to lend us the amount? Mama? He's going to lend us money?

MAITE. Sí, se ofreció.

VALERIA. Then that's great. This is great news, right?

MAITE. I don't want to talk about this, niñas! Why do people insist on ruining my day talking about this?!

> (**MAITE** *abruptly gets up and goes to the windows. She starts to open the curtains in the most dramatic of manners.)*

¿Qué no entienden las dos? This land is sacred! / ¡Mira ven para acá Anita!

VALERIA. Mama!

ANITA. Mom, you're so hardcore right now. Chill!

MAITE. Look at those trees! Vean nada más ese huerto. *[Look at that pecan orchard, just look at that orchard.]* LOOK AT IT! There is nothing more beautiful in the whole world to me. My mother is still walking in that nogalar. Our line has passed down through the women. Who in this country can say that?

ANITA. What? That the men always die?

MAITE. No, that we live if it lives! How could I slice the flesh of that orchard and sell it by the pound? For what? So that these filthy men can come and rape my trees to plant their...whatever it is they want to plant on my side of the mountain.

(*To* **VALERIA.**)

¿Memo te ha comentado algo a ti? *[Has Memo told you anything?]*

(**VALERIA** *nods her head.*)

So he and you have talked. What do you think of this... offer?

VALERIA. *(Cautious.)* I think that we are lucky to even have a choice.

MAITE. You call this a choice?! Ana Maria, do you know what this borrowed money would be for? Do you know that what these locusts want is a levy – let's call it rent – to be able to stay in our own house?

ANITA. Shutup what?!

MAITE. We would be allowed to stay in the house. But they would require unrestricted use of the orchard.

VALERIA. Mother, it's either we accept this and keep the house or we lose it all and we are homeless. I don't like it any more than you do, but if you'd seen how badly things have –

MAITE. I know how things are, Valeria! This was my house before you claimed it as yours.

VALERIA. "Before I claimed it as mine"?! / Claimed it?! I was TOLD to come here! Tú me lo informaste, Mama!

ANITA. Okay, hold on. Am I not understanding something? I thought we owed money to a bank. Wait, shut up! Listen! I thought we owed money to the bank.

VALERIA. *They* are the bank now, Ana Maria.

ANITA. Who?

VALERIA. Mama, if we don't sell it to them, they will just take it. You're not understanding.

MAITE. YOU ARE NOT UNDERSTANDING. This is my mother's house. My grandmother's pecan trees. I want to vomit just thinking about it.

VALERIA. And your daughter's pecan trees! You don't have to tell me, I have been sitting here like a guard dog for five years, Mama. A mi no me lo tienes que explicar.

 (Beat.)

ANITA. So what would happen to the nogalar?

MAITE. Who knows? Clear it, build a runway for their planes? Build a narco mansion with an eight car garage? ¿Te lo imaginas? *[Can you imagine?]* Why don't they cut out the flesh from my back instead, cut that before I let them cut down one tree.

VALERIA. They'll cut more than that, Mama. Tú decides.

MAITE. I will not even consider the notion! ¿Me entiendes? Y se acabó el tema. ¡Basta! *[Do you understand me? Subject closed. Enough.]* Do not bring this up to me again. Me voy a dar un baño. *[I'm going to take a shower.]*

 (She goes to the bathroom. Offstage.)

Towels?!

VALERIA. Debe de haber… I'll go get you some!

 (She exits.)

MAITE. *(Offstage.)* ¡Es un desmadre en esta casa! *[This house is a mess!]*

 *(**ANITA** is left alone. Suddenly.)*

ANITA. Is nobody going to feed me?!

 (She shuffles out.)

End of Scene

Scene Seven

(A day later. The playroom. **LOPEZ** *is fixing a drawer in the big bookcase.* **DUNIA** *enters. She's eating a messy pecan candy [Besos Indios].* **LOPEZ** *hits his head when* **DUNIA** *calls out his name.)*

DUNIA. MEMO!

(Hits his head.)

Aguas, que te sale un chichon, eh. *[Watch it, you'll get a bump.]*

(She turns off the light. [English].)

You can't have the light on like this; you know who will come on her broomstick.

LOPEZ. Don't be ridiculous, how am I supposed to fix this in pure darkness?

DUNIA. Don't exaggerate. Look at all this sun.

LOPEZ. Turn it back on.

DUNIA. You turn it on.

LOPEZ. I'm not playing with you.

DUNIA. I'm not playing with you.

LOPEZ. Little brat. Always been a little brat.

DUNIA. Hey, I'm just the enforcer. I'm a good girl, I do what I'm told.

LOPEZ. Good girl my left...ear. What is that you're eating? Gross.

(Beat.)

Always like a little kid...

DUNIA. *(She fully enters the room.)* So when are these wedded nuptials supposed to happen, huh? We're all waiting to buy the present already. I was going to get you matching belt buckles.

LOPEZ. I'm almost positive that you have something better to do than to be talking nonsense to me.

DUNIA. No.

(He goes back under the cabinet.)

LOPEZ. There's nothing you should be doing right now? Helping somebody with something?

DUNIA. Nope. Everybody's gone. They went off to the cascade.

LOPEZ. *(Comes back up and hits his head.)* Ah, fuck.

(Beat.)

They left already?

DUNIA. They left already.

LOPEZ. I was going to take them, I told them I would take them. That I'd go with them.

DUNIA. Well, they left you.

*(A moment as **DUNIA** sucks on her pecan candy; it's a little messy.)*

LOPEZ. Ugh, go find something to do.

DUNIA. Hey, don't get angry at me because they left you. I didn't leave you.

(Beat.)

They left me too, you know. We went this morning from: "Oh, yes, let's all go bathe in the cascade! Let's have a picnic," to: "Pack our things in the car Dunia, see you tonight when we get back." What kind of wishy-washy thing is that? So annoying, all of them. Like nothing or nobody matters but them.

(Beat.)

Remember when you and Martin and everybody used to go to the cascade for the day?

LOPEZ. When did they leave?

DUNIA. Not twenty minutes ago. You didn't hear them? I was wondering why you kept working on that thing.

LOPEZ. The screws are oxidized. The nails too. This thing is really old, I don't want to cause too much damage so I was / taking my time.

DUNIA. Can I ask you a question, Memo?

(Beat.)

Why are you fixing their cabinet?

LOPEZ. Go make me something to eat, will you.

DUNIA. You act like the foreman, always with your tools. You're not a carpenter anymore.

LOPEZ. Hey, what you learn early in life, you never forget. That's why you should learn something useful, little girl.

DUNIA. I just don't understand it.

LOPEZ. Go get me something to eat, Dunia.

(She offers him a pecan candy.)

Don't be sassy. You know I don't have a sweet tooth. Go make me something salty. Those gorditas your mom makes, can you make those?

DUNIA. I'm just never going to understand it. Is it because you want to impress Valeria? Listen, you don't have to work too hard with her.

(Beat.)

Well, I don't want to make your head swell. But what do you see in her anyway?

(Pause.)

LOPEZ. Her eyes. They're like her mother's but deeper. She's got the kindest eyes of any woman. She's a good person.

DUNIA. So what are you waiting for?

LOPEZ. You know what? I'm going to finish this later. Your yapping is giving me a stomachache. I liked it better when you weren't talking to me.

(Beat.)

Come on. I'm kidding. I'm just hungry here, but you won't feed me so I'm leaving.

(He starts to go.)

DUNIA. Wait, don't go. I don't want to stay here all...by myself. Stay and keep me company. I came up to ask you a question anyway, a favor.

LOPEZ. What is it now?

DUNIA. Will you teach me the Internet?

LOPEZ. What do you mean? Show you how to use it?

DUNIA. Yes, will you teach me how it works? I want to know how to work it.

LOPEZ. I don't know. You'd be trouble on the Internet. Next thing we know you'll sell yourself off as an order bride. End up in Russia or some place. Married to some old pervert.

DUNIA. You can do that?

LOPEZ. Hhhmm...the Internet is too dangerous for you. Or better yet, you're too dangerous for the Internet.

DUNIA. You know what? Forget it. I thought maybe you of all people would want me to learn something new...do something with myself. People just want to keep you down and keep you stupid. Everybody saying the same thing. "Stop dreaming so much, Dunia." Everyone's got a plan for you when you had no say in making it. People writing out your story before you even have a chance to pick up a pen and write something yourself. People are like flies in a jar.

LOPEZ. Did you say "flies in a jar"?

DUNIA. I thought maybe you of all people would let me at least think about...*wanting* to think –

LOPEZ. Flies in a jar, huh?

DUNIA. Just forget it.

LOPEZ. Alright, I'll teach you! I'll teach you. Oh, man you're like a little tiger, aren't you? You turned into a little tiger right before my eyes and I hadn't even noticed.

DUNIA. Shut up.

LOPEZ. I'll help you. Come on.

DUNIA. Really?

LOPEZ. Yeah, come on, let's go. We'll start with Google.

> *(Beat.)*

Oh, man. We are all going to regret this aren't we?

> *(They exit.)*

End of Scene

Scene Eight

*(The next day. Just outside the house, on something like a porch. Late afternoon. **VALERIA**'s been trying to make cabrito. She's a little sweaty, wearing an apron. Trying not to be a hot mess.)*

VALERIA. Dunia! Dunia! Where the devil are you? Dunia! I swear…she turns more and more unruly with each day… Dunia!

*(**DUNIA** enters.)*

DUNIA. I'm not deaf. I kept saying that "I'm coming. I'M COMING. / I'm coming." You can't hear me because you keep shouting, "DUNIA! DUNIA."

VALERIA. Where in the devil did you go and hide? I've been calling you – looking for you all over the house. You know there's only you and Fulgencio now. But he can barely stand. STOP DISAPPEARING.

DUNIA. I've been here.

VALERIA. Do not tell me lies. / Where were you?

DUNIA. I'm not.

(To herself.) Shoot me in the head.

VALERIA. I'm not going to tell you again about how you talk to me. I demand that you treat me as I should be treated.

(Beat.)

DUNIA. Did you need me for something?

VALERIA. You know, this past month you've developed a smart mouth on you and started running off to who knows where. Where do you go?! Do your job!

DUNIA. I'm sorry. I'm here now.

VALERIA. Dunia, if you end up in a ditch somewhere –

DUNIA. I will never end up in a ditch.

VALERIA. Dunia, do not tempt fate.

(Pause.)

You think that I don't like you or that I don't worry about you.

DUNIA. You worry about me?

VALERIA. Dunia. Yes, of course, I worry about you.

DUNIA. Maybe better to worry about yourself in this house all alone.

VALERIA. Well, I'm not all alone anymore, am I? We have two very demanding guests who have insisted that we make them goat. In the traditional buried style, no less. Ah, this heat! It's cooking my brain!

DUNIA. It's because you're right by the fire.

VALERIA. I know.

DUNIA. Memo's here already. He seemed very excited about the goat. Right outside the gates.

VALERIA. Did he stay out there talking to those men again?

DUNIA. Yeah, but it's just Pedro. Just them two out there. Oh, and the Señora Maite.

VALERIA. What!

DUNIA. The Señora Maite. She's out there with them two. She brought out a tequila and they're there drinking it. They've almost gone through the whole barrel.

VALERIA. *(Frozen in a panic, pause before she says to herself.)* Please God, protect us...

DUNIA. They're fine. They're not doing anything. They were all three of them laughing and even singing a couple of songs. They were talking about the government / and who knows what.

VALERIA. The what? Oh, God no no no...

DUNIA. They're fine. Nothing bad is happening.

VALERIA. OF COURSE SOMETHING BAD IS HAPPENING! I'm making the fucking goat! Why my mother got it in her head to eat goat, I will never know. Wasn't she a vegetarian? In my life have we ever made goat. In my life!

DUNIA. It smells good though. You're good to make it for them. You are.

(Beat.)

VALERIA. I think it's smoking too much. I wouldn't know, I've never seen it made. Five years ago, I never would have been here making goat. Five years ago, someone… Tere or someone…would have been making the goat and I would have been sitting by the gates enjoying aged tequila with everybody… Wait, no I wouldn't. Proper guests don't sit by the gates drinking anejo. This can't be a good thing this little party of theirs out there.

> *(**ANITA** enters.)*

ANITA. Okay, if I have to watch Mami *accidentally* pull up her skirt again to fan herself when she laughs, when she's really just showing off her legs, I will proceed to barf. She's over there flirting with those two. Oooh, what's that smell, it smells so good.

VALERIA. It's not ready. At least, I don't think it is… Is Mami talking to Pedro?

> *(**ANITA** nods.)*

She shouldn't be talking to Pedro at all.

ANITA. No, it's fine. They're going down memory lane.

VALERIA. Ah, Mami thinks she can just let down her hair and say any old thing. I should go get her.

ANITA. Don't. She's laughing and not inventing dramas. Gambling relaxes her.

VALERIA. What do you mean gambling? With money?

ANITA. I think…yeah, with money. Oh, what. Don't get crazy.

VALERIA. She's over there gambling our money away?! Is she simple in the head?! Please tell me because I need to know! Doesn't she see that I'M THE ONE WHO HAS TO MAKE THE GOAT?

> *(She takes off her apron and starts to exit to go do some damage control.)*

ANITA. The what?

VALERIA. Dunia, watch the goat.

> *(Exits.)*

DUNIA. Watch the goat? What am I watching it do?

ANITA. Why does she keep it so dark out here too? Where are the lights, Dunia? For out here?

DUNIA. Right here.

> *(She turns on the lights outside. They nicely light up the porch. Something dreamy about them. [Translation: English/Spanish].)*

Sí es que a ella le duele el codo. Everything hurts her elbow. No, that is not the manner how you say it in English. How do you say que es bien tacaña? *[How do you say that she's stingy?]* How do you say in English?

ANITA. Stingy. She's not stingy, she just needs to keep us all… Hey! Hello. Pedro?

DUNIA. ¿Pedro qué?

ANITA. He was basically twitching for you. Couldn't concentrate on what he was saying.

DUNIA. Yes, he twitches but that's because se mete that mierda.

> *(She pretends to sniff cocaine.)*

Ay, él es un…he's such a dumb. Killing his neuronas. Neuronas are neurons?

ANITA. Brain cells. I don't think he's dumb at all. A little tweaked out though maybe.

DUNIA. Not dumb pero… Es que parece moco. He doesn't leave me in peace, he's a piece of gum in my shoe. I'm hoping que se le pase and moves on to pursuing another girl. It gives me a little bit of fear to say no to him since he does have a little bad temper.

ANITA. You know I used to have a crush on him, right?

DUNIA. Oh, I'm sorry.

ANITA. Oh, please, no…like when I was ten. When I was ten!

DUNIA. Pos, he does not match you. You're not of the same...son "de distintas sociedades" como dice Selena.

ANITA. That is the stupidest thing I've ever heard.

DUNIA. You didn't like Selena?

ANITA. No, just the whole...

> *(Beat.)*

DUNIA. Tienes razón. *[You're right.]* Pedro is not so bad idea for now. He is better than the dumb one I was going out with before, more handsome than this poor little counter I was going with. Is that how you say contador?

ANITA. Isn't it accountant?

DUNIA. Ah, yes. Accountant. Not counter. Sí, ese era todo un ñoño. Who wants a ñoño? How you say ñoño?

ANITA. I don't know...ah, mama's boy? No, I don't know.

DUNIA. I need a real man. Who wants a ñoño like that? Imaginate. We will start getting into kissing and he will faint and have an attack from excitement. Así que lo pusimos de patitas en la calle. *[So we kicked him to the curb.]* Good bye, baby.

ANITA. How do you do it? I wish I had your... I don't know how you call it. I turn stupid in front of guys. They scare me. Everything scares me lately.

> *(Beat.)*

I need a pedicure.

DUNIA. Men are easy. There is not one easier animal on the planet than a man.

ANITA. Oooh, Dunia.

DUNIA. I'm not being a bad person when I say this. So yes las feministas who like to say progressive things on the morning shows. They will speak to us about equality and things like this. Pero no. Men are stupid animals. They are smart, but they are stupid animals. Esto de lidiar con ellos es fácil. *[Dealing with them is easy.]* But only if you have...moneda con que negociar. *[currency to trade.]*

ANITA. What does that mean?

DUNIA. You have to have…something they want. And no I'm not talking about sex. That only lasts three minutes and that's all you got. You lose them after they're done. No, I'm talking something else. Like to possess. Men like to know they are masters and owners of you. And you must let them know that this is so. Even if it is a lie.

ANITA. Nobody will be the master and owner of me, Dunia.

DUNIA. Then you will never find happiness with a man.

(Quickly and pleased.)

Uy, my English has gotten so good since you came this week.

ANITA. What you are saying is so backwards it's not even funny. If you knew what you sound like –

DUNIA. No, for pretend. You only must let them think that you are something to be won. You make a face at me, but you profoundly know it is true. This is what our mothers and grandmothers teach us from always and we stop listening because we say we are modern, but they are always correct.

ANITA. My mother never taught me anything like that. But that's not saying much. My mother hasn't really tried to teach me much of anything.

(Beat.)

God, she's a mess. I don't want to be a mess… I think that if I would have grown up properly, you know, here in this house, in one place like I was supposed to. With my dad and my mom, not from boarding school to boarding school I think –

(Beat.)

I'm talking too much.

DUNIA. No, para nada. Yo soy una tumba. *[No, not at all. Let it all out. I'm a tomb.]*

(She zips her mouth.)

ANITA. I love my mother.

DUNIA. I know. Even not being here fifteen years everybody loves your mother. She was the most beautiful girl in these parts everyone says.

ANITA. I know! Trust me, you do not have to remind me. That's what everyone's told me ever since I can remember. So shitty to always have to be compared to her. Poor Vale really hated it. Because she was first and when she wasn't...you know, when she wasn't all like my mom and like...sparkly, then everybody just kind of gave up on her. It's like everybody just kind of gave up on her early on. But me? Everyone has such high expectations from me. About whom I'll marry and who my friends will be, it's all so paralyzing. But where I've ended up there isn't this Mexican prince I'm going to meet, with the right pedigree and the right credentials.

> *(Beat.)*

What is the right pedigree anyway? What are people holding on to? This country – I'm sorry but from where I stand it looks like it's falling apart. Just like this house; it's falling apart. And I'm going to say something really shitty but... I kind of don't care if we keep this place. That's shitty to say, but what does it really mean to me, you know? I don't feel welcomed here. Everything – even those trees look at me with resentment. So fuck it. I know I'm being shitty right now. But ever since we got here, everyone's shoving the whole "you're home" thing down my throat... I don't know. I guess I am being a little shitty.

> *(MAITE and VALERIA enter. Poor VALERIA. She's on the verge of tears.)*

MAITE. Esos dos quedaron pero bien... They are completely and absolutely gone. I mean, I don't believe we will get them to come to the house for dinner tonight. They will probably pass out.

> *(Beat.)*

Oye, que bien se expresa Pedro, ¿no? He's smart and eloquent and I like how he talks. But our poor Memo. The words he uses. What a little dummy, Dios Mio.

(Beat.)

That smells delicious, Vale!

VALERIA. Mami, yo que tú no me comería ese cabrito, I don't think I prepared it properly. *[Mom, if I were you I wouldn't have any of that goat, I don't know if I prepared it properly.]*

(She sits down.)

MAITE. Nonsense, it smells wonderful!

ANITA. (To VALERIA.) What's the matter with you?

VALERIA. (Bursting into tears.) Nothing.

MAITE. Dios, siempre de Magdalena. *[God, always a weeping Magdalena.]* Valeria, you're a puddle of tears everywhere you go. I am so sorry. I should have consulted you. Here, let's go get my purse and have you hold it. I don't ever want to see it. From now on you keep it. Mi amorcito, please stop crying. You're going to make me feel so guilty.

VALERIA. I just don't understand you. It's like you don't care.

MAITE. Sweetheart, of course I care. What are you talking about?

VALERIA. Mami, no tenemos ni para la luz. *[Mom, we don't even have enough to pay the light bill.]* They're going to cut it any moment.

(Pause.)

Dunia, ¿nos puedes dejar solas por favor? *[Dunia, will you leave us please?]*

MAITE. No, Dunia is family, ¿verdad Dunia? No seas grocera, Vale. *[Don't be rude, Vale.]* Just say it. Estamos en confianza. *[We're amongst friends.]*

VALERIA. We can barely pay Dunia!

ANITA. Are we serious?

MAITE. Anita, it's not as bad as all that. Valeria is always enveloped in a cloud of despair. No lo tomes tan en serio. *[Don't take it so seriously.]*

ANITA. Vale, for real?

VALERIA. We owe everybody. And there's nothing, nothing left.

MAITE. Jesus Christ! Such drama.

ANITA. Mami, are you listening? They're going to cut off the electricity! We can't even afford the necessities, like Dunia. Like a cook to cook this thing…

MAITE. Memo will help us. Él nos va a prestar una cantidad, ya / me lo prometio. *[He's going to lend us a sum, he's already promised.]*

ANITA. Oh, thank God.

VALERIA. ¿De verdad?

> *(Beat.)*

You're going to accept their offer and let him give you the money?

MAITE. Sure. Yes. I'm speaking with him tonight, tomorrow. I'll speak with him.

VALERIA. Ay, gracias a Dios.

MAITE. Girls, everything will work itself out, I'm sure of it.

ANITA. Mom, this is not something that you can just make up a story about, like with my tuition. This is serious shit. Are you really talking to him? I know how you are.

MAITE. Anita, tomorrow I'll talk to him, ¿te parece? We will come to an agreement. Okay? I just don't want everyone to get so worked up and worried and bursting into tears at the drop of a hat and full of ulcers and wrinkles because then we'll never be able to marry you off. Please, Vale. Please, for me. You want me to do a little dance for you? Mira te bailo para que sonrías. ¿Cuál te bailo? *[Look I'll dance for you so that you smile. Which one should I dance for you?]*

ANITA. Great, now she's going to start dancing. Here we go…

(**MAITE** *sings two verses of "El Sauce Y La Palma."**)

(*Beat.*)

MAITE. My mother would sing that song up and down the corridors of this house. Tan alegre, mi madre. *[Such a happy woman, my mother.]* Because back then there was nothing to worry about. We had the sky and the air and the world and it was all ours, and there was nothing to worry about. Eran tiempos tan bellos. *[And you felt such peace throughout this land.]*

(*Beat.*)

Baila conmigo, Ana Maria. *[Dance with me, Ana Maria.]*

ANITA. Sorry, no. How do you even dance to that?

MAITE. You are no daughter of mine. ¿Vale? ¿Bailamos? No esta, menos. *[Want to dance? No, much less this one.]* My two daughters the statues. Tú Dunia. Ándale, tú sí que eres alegre. *[You Dunia, you are a happy soul.]*

(**DUNIA** *dances with her throughout the next exchange.* **DUNIA** *hums the song.*)

Ántes habia un conjunto por aquí, they used to come and play for your dinners or parties. We should have a party.

DUNIA. Ay, sí. Eso estaría muy bien, oiga. *[Oh, yes. That would be very nice.]*

VALERIA. (*Under her breath.*) …Nadie vendría. *[No one would come.]*

MAITE. What did you say?

(**MAITE** *and* **DUNIA** *continue to dance.*)

---

*A license to produce *Mala Hierba* does not include a performance license for "El Sauce Y La Palma." The publisher and author suggest that the licensee contact ASCAP or BMI to ascertain the music publisher and contact such music publisher to license or acquire permission for performance of the song. If a license or permission is unattainable for "El Sauce Y La Palma" the licensee may not use the song in *Mala Hierba* but may create an original composition in a similar style. For further information, please see Music Use Note on page 3.

VALERIA. No one would come, Mama. There's no one left and if there is someone left, we probably owe them money so they wouldn't want to come. That's just the truth! ¡Nadie vendría! *[No one would come.]*

> *(The cabrito starts to smoke and spark. The women react. It has a little bit of a firecracker effect.* **VALERIA** *is hysterical,* **ANITA** *tries to help. They are running around and very vocally collaborating in the extinguishing of the fire.* **MAITE** *develops a slow rising laughing fit as the women run around to put out the sparks. They calm the sparks and smoke and all we hear is* **MAITE** *laughing a cackle. Is she crying too? Who knows, but she's going through a Thing. More laughter. The women are astounded, staring at her.)*

MAITE. …IT'S… IT'S ALL GOING UP IN FLAMES. DO WE HAVE INSURANCE?

…MAYBE… MAYBE THAT'S THE ANSWER. ¡QUE SE ENCIENDA TODO! ¡HASTA EL NOGALAR! EVERYTHING…

> *(Laughter.)*

IT'S ALL GOING UP IN FLAMES…

> *(All we hear is her laughter. The others are dumbfounded. Smoke.)*

End of Scene

Scene Nine

*(Outside. **LOPEZ** is by a makeshift campfire, out by the gate. There is a sea of bottles of Negra Modelo and Pacífico and a barrel of tequila. He starts to put them into a trash bag, the trash which their little gathering has produced.)*

LOPEZ. See, this is good. This is progress.

(Drinks from his beer.)

What is all they're burning over there?

(He waves away smoke.)

This is progress. We are not reduced to being fucking animals when we hold civilized, what, discourse. Civilized discourse. Maite has always been so civilized.

(Beat.)

It's funny. When I was a kid, you wouldn't have dared to sit by a fire, out in the open criticizing the government. But now, nobody cares. What are they going to do to us? This government is a pack of toothless dogs now. Yeah, they can bark, but who are they going to bite? Those rabid wolves up on that mountain? I don't think so.

(Beat.)

"The world of men is a broken toy," like Pedro just said. Smart guy, that guy. I'm glad it's him they have on watch. It could have been anybody Chato put on Los Nogales. And in these times of the Four Horsemen. In these times, decent men turn into beasts. Beasts that have been watching you, waiting to descend to pillage and burn everything to ash. I've seen them do it. This place doesn't deserve that end. Am I the only one who still loves those trees?

(Beat.)

My life is written out in the bark of those pecans. That orchard is the first thing I can remember. Me running around with no shoes, carrying those baskets of pecans back to the silos.

(Beat.)

Oh, man. Beer and tequila don't mix.

(A queasy moment.)

When I was like, I don't know how old, old enough to feel like I was a full-grown man, my father gave me one of those beatings that break off a bit of your soul. The old man was taking out a whole day of frustrations on my back. Going at it hard as he could with that whip when out of nowhere Maite appears and pushes him off me. She gives him one hard slap on his leather face. She curses something at him and then drags me with her to the silos. She says, "Don't cry little man." I'm standing there in front of her, bleeding, shaking. And slowly, very slowly she takes off my shirt. Then she starts to hose me down. "Don't cry, little man," she says even when I had stopped crying.

(Pause.)

Shit, after that, I followed her like a puppy. Too old to be doing that and I know her parents had said something to her. Well, because she was just divorced and with a kid and well, it wasn't proper. But she didn't care and I didn't care. We went everywhere together. We…

(Beat.)

One day, I guess it was when her father found her the new husband. That day she took me from cracking pecans, and…she just took me by the river to this little wall the bank makes. She'd been crying. She said, "Take off your clothes, little man." Oh, man, I took off my pants so fast. Almost fell in the water. She starts laughing and takes off her dress. I have never… I have never seen something more beautiful in my whole life. With that light that day. With the sun on her. And all of her just standing there. And me tangled on the ground with my fucking pants. She says, "Stay there, little man.

You can look at me, but you can't touch." So I freeze there. Looking. For I don't know how long. Then she pulls up her dress and runs. She ran so fast, so fast that she left her sandals there. When I went up to the house to give them to her the next morning they said she was gone. That she'd gone off to live in Monterrey where she was going to be married. Just like that, they took her away from me.

(Pause.)

Me and these trees, we're the only ones who remember. Right by that river there. Not far from the bank. "You can look, but you can't touch."

> (**LOPEZ** *throws the trash bag down, which he's been holding. He fumbles for his keys and presses the keyless start. He stumbles off.*)

End of Scene

Scene Ten

(VALERIA is in the playroom. She's wearing her version of a party dress; we can hear the music from the party outside. She's pacing.)

VALERIA. This music!

(MAITE enters, helping ANITA into the room. ANITA is a little drunk; she's carrying a bottle of tequila and is protesting as MAITE tries to take it away. MAITE finds ANITA's drunkenness amusing.)

MAITE. A ver. Dáme esto. Give me that, Ana Maria. / Look at her, who knew she was such a lightweight.

ANITA. This tequila is a hundred years old. / Can you believe it? One hundred years…

MAITE. She got into your father's anejo. I just took it out so we could toast, not so you would – Calmadita. / Let's sit you down right here.

ANITA. Now, you don't want to dance, Mami?

MAITE. Let's get you some water. Valeria, pásame ese botella por favor.

(VALERIA serves ANITA some water.)

VALERIA. What is taking Memo so long?! He left in the afternoon. I wish he'd just call. He could call us and let us know something. God, please be alright. Si algo le pasa… No, he'll be fine. He's fine.

MAITE. Of course he'll be fine. Why wouldn't he be fine? I think all this will be pretty standard. He'll make them our offer and lend us the money every month until we get up on our feet.

VALERIA. And what's the plan then, Mamá? To get up on our feet?

(A sobering moment between **MAITE** *and* **VALERIA** *as* **ANITA** *attempts to stand up and dance.)*

ANITA. Let's get up on our feet and dance! I may not be able to talk Mexican but I can dance Mexican, look!

MAITE. Here, let's drink. A ti sólo te damos un dedito, Anis, porque si no – / But we should toast. I brought it out so we would toast.

(Grabs the tequila.)

Valeria's father brought this for me from Jalisco when we got married. We will drink it in a proper glass, not in one of those horrendous shot glasses the gringos drink out of. This is sipping tequila. No chaser here.

ANITA. Just a little finger. Just this much, look, this much.

(Beat.)

*(***MAITE** *has served* **VALERIA** *a glass; she refuses.)*

VALERIA. No thank you.

MAITE. It's your father's tequila, Valeria.

*(***VALERIA** *takes it.)*

To the women.

ANITA. And dancing.

MAITE. Valeria?

VALERIA. To home.

MAITE. Yes, to our nogalar. The most beautiful orchard in all of Mexico.

ANITA. Aaajua!

(They drink and have some laughter and levity. A car is heard outside in the midst of the music.)

VALERIA. *(She looks out the window.)* It's Memo!

MAITE. *(To* **VALERIA.***)* No, let me. Stay here.

(**MAITE** *runs out. The song changes from a lively cumbia, to a corrido, "No Mas Las Mujeres Quedan."***)

ANITA. There's a lot of dudes downstairs. What, don't we know any women?

VALERIA. I told Mami no one would come. We have no friends left. Puros nacos y narcos, Ana Maria. Those are wolves downstairs. Ten years ago the governor would have been downstairs. Senators and proper people. Ahora nada más ve esto. Qué vergüenza. *[How embarrassing.]* Oh, God! What could Memo be telling her? I'm going downstairs.

ANITA. Valeria, wait. Will you teach me how to dance to this song? Nobody's ever taught me. There are so many things I know half way. Like I know the beginning or the ending, but I don't know the middle. I'm a half person, Vale. I walk around incomplete. My tongue is a half tongue, my brain too. I'm a half thing.

VALERIA. Mi pobre Anita.

(A moment of tenderness.)

You know, I have a suspicion that we were meant to be happy people but it just didn't pan out that way, did it?

ANITA. We are happy people now. Memo is fixing everything.

(**MAITE** *shrieks offstage/in this darkened area. She is throwing curses at* **LOPEZ** *and hitting him, he's trying to calm her. This is all in Spanish.)*

Whoa, what was that?

**A license to produce *Mala Hierba* does not include a performance license for "No Mas Las Mujeres Quedan." The publisher and author suggest that the licensee contact ASCAP or BMI to ascertain the music publisher and contact such music publisher to license or acquire permission for performance of the song. If a license or permission is unattainable for "No Mas Las Mujeres Quedan" the licensee may not use the song in *Mala Hierba* but may create an original composition in a similar style. For further information, please see Music Use Note on page 3.

VALERIA. NO, DON'T GO. Dios Santo.

> (**MAITE** *runs upstairs in a fit to the master bedroom. The girls follow her into that room. She is madly taking things out of the closet, starting to pack. She is making guttural noises like a beast. She's a red-eyed beast right now. The first few lines overlap.*)

MAMÁ, ¿QUÉ TE DIJO?

ANITA. Mami, what happened?

MAITE. Nefasto!

> (*Beat.*)

Pelele! /

> (*Beat.*)

¡Cabrón hijo de su puta madre!

VALERIA. Mama, ¿qué pasó con Los Nogales?

MAITE. What Los Nogales!

VALERIA. Mama por favor! ¿Qué pasó?!

MAITE. We have no Nogales, Valeria! It's all gone!

ANITA. But Memo went to talk to them for us.

MAITE. Did he? Or did he go talk to them for him?

VALERIA. Mamá...

MAITE. ¿Sabes qué hizo ese hijo de puta? Your Memo, tu Memin Pinguin, bought it whole. They wouldn't take a monthly payoff so El Señor Lopez bought it himself! This whole time walking around here, en confianza. / Us treating him like family! ¡ES UNA PINCHE VIBORA!

VALERIA. No. / No. No...

ANITA. Memo? Why would he do that?

MAITE. WHY WOULD HE DO THAT? Because he's waited twenty years to do that, that's why.

> (*She is a fiend packing while* **VALERIA** *talks.*)

VALERIA. I mean, if we get married, maybe we can just stay here, you know? Mejor no me Adelanto. Does this mean we have a bit of money, now? Yes, this means that we'll be able to at least live on it for a time. We could get a flat in Monterrey and I'll figure out what to do. I will… I will get a job. I can translate, I'll do that. I know four languages and how to do accounting. I'm sure I can find something. Anita, you will go to school somewhere in Monterrey and everything will be alright. Don't cry, Anis. Todo va a estar bien.

ANITA. Why would he do that to us? I don't understand…

MAITE. *(This is a different* **MAITE,** *no theatrics here.)* That little man. Ese pinchee indio pata rajada. / This man who wouldn't have been allowed to set a foot inside this house now owns my nogalar!

VALERIA. ¡MAMÁ! No digas burradas! He must have done this for a reason. I trust him.

MAITE. Don't trust in this hijo the puta so much, mi hija. You don't know this man the way I know this man.

ANITA. Mami, please stop talking right now.

MAITE. You think he's the Memo who fixed our cars when you were growing up? The Memo who built those benches on the porch? The Memo who was ready and willing to lend a helping hand whenever you called him? You think that's who this Memo is?

ANITA. Mami, please!

MAITE. You better thank the heavens that he was never interested enough to marry you, Valeria.

ANITA. Mother, stop! I fucking mean it, don't be a fucking bitch right now. / If you do this, I swear I'll never fucking speak to you again.

MAITE. What?! You would let your sister marry a man who's been absolutely obsessed with her mother for, what, twenty years? You'd want that for your sister? A man who followed me to Monterrey when I was marrying your father and stood outside of our new house for almost a fucking month just looking up at our window. Anywhere I went, there he was. Salivating for me, like a little animal. Devouring me with those two eyes. I had to convince your father to move us to Guadalajara to get away from him because he was absolutely obsessed with me. He's been obsessed with me for twenty fucking years. This little man. This little animal! And now he owns my orchard! He finally got what he's always... Ahora es amo y patrón de los Nogales. *[Now he's lord and master of Los Nogales.]*

ANITA. You're unbelievable.

MAITE. Ay, ya. Era hora de que lo supiera. *[Oh, enough. It was time you knew the truth.]*

> (VALERIA *goes to her mother. She takes off the keys from her waist and throws them on the floor. She is stone. Nothing left.*)

ANITA. Vale...

> (VALERIA *darts a look at* ANITA *as she exits.*)

You're a hateful person. A mean bitch, that's all you are.

> (MAITE *is a sitting lump on the floor.*)

You...you don't even care what happens to the three of us, do you?

> (ANITA *exits, following after* VALERIA. MAITE *is left there. So alone.*)

End of Scene

Scene Eleven

(LOPEZ *is outside. He's obviously been celebrating.*
He carries a flashlight and a bottle of tequila.
He's elated beyond words and doesn't know what
to do with himself. He points at the sky with the
flashlight, all around him, at his face. A million
thoughts run through his head. The large flashlight
starts to go out on him.)

LOPEZ. Puta madre!

(*As the flashlight dies,* DUNIA *enters. [Translated*
World].)

DUNIA. It's alright. You don't need that. The stars shine
bright enough for you tonight.

LOPEZ. Don't they?

DUNIA. You're going to have to sleep here, you know?
You're in no state to drive home.

LOPEZ. Look at them stars.

DUNIA. Although, what am I saying? You get to sleep here
from now on if you want. I just heard.

LOPEZ. No one would shake my hand.

DUNIA. How are they going to shake your hand and the
Galvan women are all still here?

LOPEZ. I tried to warn them…

DUNIA. Of what? That you were planning to screw them
out of house and home?

LOPEZ. Don't say that like that –

DUNIA. Wait, I didn't mean it like that.

LOPEZ. Just don't say it that way. That's not how it was. I
went to Chato and repeated every word Maite said, like
a parrot. But he was not in a good mood. He just…
I knew as soon as I got there that things wouldn't – I
said, we will give you this much if you let them stay. He
laughed in the way he laughs right before he's going to
shoot somebody. So that's when I blurt out, "Chato, I'll

give you my warehouses and the three gas stations. I'll give you half of everything I own if you let me keep the nogalar. Well, he stopped laughing then.

(He laughs.)

It was like someone else was speaking through my mouth. Next thing I knew, Los Nogales was mine.

(Beat.)

Los Nogales is mine, Dunia. Can you believe that?

DUNIA. No.

LOPEZ. But she, she won't hear of it. She won't even consider staying here. I would let her stay here. My father...if my father could see me now. If my grandfather, who didn't even speak Spanish. He spoke in dialect. He was a poor Indian from the mountains, if my grandfather could see me now. / Oh, man, I'm not breathing right. There's like a boulder on my chest.

DUNIA. Here, sit down.

LOPEZ. No, I'm alright...

DUNIA. Here, just sit down. Sit down I say.

(They struggle but he sits.)

LOPEZ. When did you get to be so bossy?

DUNIA. Now I'm bossy because I don't want you to fall on your big ugly face?

LOPEZ. ...Yes.

DUNIA. Fine, then I'll be bossy. Are you feeling better?

LOPEZ. I'm fine.

(Pause.)

DUNIA. Are you still...you and Valeria? Do you think she'll still...

LOPEZ. Oh, shit. I better go find her.

DUNIA. I hope Valeria still wants to be your wife.

LOPEZ. God, I hope so too.

DUNIA. But do you think... I mean, do you think she would now? Marry you? After what you did to them?

LOPEZ. …

DUNIA. Valeria, she can't stand beside you. Even if she wanted to. She's not like you.

LOPEZ. Valeria's a saint. Ah, man. I should go talk to her.

(Getting up to go.)

DUNIA. No, no, wait. Wait… Right now she needs to be up there with her mother and Ana. Leave her alone for a bit. Trust me, you're probably the last person she wants to see right now.

LOPEZ. Don't say that. I need to talk to her.

DUNIA. Talk to her later. Talk to her tomorrow. Look up at these stars with me. You know, you're right. They seem brighter tonight for some reason.

(They contemplate for a bit.)

You know, you shouldn't feel bad. All you've tried to do is help her out – You were ready with your open wallet.

LOPEZ. I know! I was going to lend them the money. Shit, I would have *given* them the money. Here, take it.

DUNIA. I know you would have.

LOPEZ. But they didn't listen.

DUNIA. They didn't listen and now look what happens. But that's a lesson for them, not for you.

LOPEZ. *(He turns to really look at her for the first time.)* How old are you? You sound like a full-grown adult right now.

DUNIA. Guillermo Lopez, I've been grown for a while now, you know?

(Pause.)

They deserve it a little bit, if you ask me.

LOPEZ. Don't say shit like that.

DUNIA. Uh, they don't deserve it? Even just a little?

LOPEZ. No.

(Somehow, who knows how, DUNIA will end up on LOPEZ' lap by the end of the following. It takes her the whole monologue to rope him in.)

DUNIA. Okay, maybe you should feel a little bad because they trusted you and here you went and did this thing to them. But I don't feel bad, not one little bit. These people, they've been the keepers of something that maybe wasn't theirs to keep in the first place. And we all let them have it. We even kept it for them, even as the maña got stronger and stronger all around us. They didn't have to deal with their brothers being shot, with their houses being burned. It fills me with poison to think that they can leave and come back whenever they want, when we've had to stay here guarding their things. It's never cost them anything. Well it's costing them now, isn't it? Now they'll be just like everybody else.

LOPEZ. I think if I don't talk to Valeria now, she will not –

> (**DUNIA** kisses **LOPEZ**. He's a little stunned, but it's not unwelcome.)

DUNIA. Someone should take care of you. Stand beside you.

> (She holds out her hand to shake his.)

LOPEZ. What are you doing?

DUNIA. I'm shaking your hand.

> (A moment. He shakes her hand. She pulls him and kisses him again.)

You did a brave thing, Memo. Who better than you to make something of this place?

LOPEZ. Right? This is what I was trying to explain to Maite but she kept hitting my face.

DUNIA. El Nogalar is in good hands.

LOPEZ. Yes. Exactly. I'll keep it safe until this whole occupation passes over. I know how to keep it safe.

DUNIA. No, don't do that, Memo! Don't be their little guard dog anymore. This is all yours now.

LOPEZ. I know! Fuck. It's mine. Fuck.

DUNIA. Memo, maybe the right idea now is not to leave up north anymore. We keep looking up, in hope of miracles, but maybe the miracles are right here beneath our feet. No one ever thought you would be the owner of Los Nogales. Not in a million years!

LOPEZ. No, nobody.

DUNIA. And look at you now?

LOPEZ. Yeah, look at me now…

DUNIA. Going up to the other side. Maybe that's what people had to do before, but now it's different. Maybe what we should be doing is staying here and looking down at our feet. Looking at our hands. Staying here to take what hasn't ever been ours but which has always belonged to us.

LOPEZ. She said, "You can look but you can't touch."

DUNIA. *(Kneeling between his legs, grabbing dirt.)* She did. And now look at us. Just look at us.

> *(Grabbing handfuls of dirt.)*

We can touch.

> *(She is between his legs, he can't help but be aroused. I mean, she's right there. It's obvious what she's suggesting. They kind of go at it on the ground.* **DUNIA** *is in control, but she lets him have his way a couple of times as the lights go down. An interpretive sound of trees falling. Now don't go cueing chainsaws because it's not literal. Just make me feel trees are falling. Along with the upper class. Ting. Ting. TONG. Goodbye to the bed of Porfirio Díaz.)*

End of Play